Judged For Revenge

By David Evans

Table of Contents

Chapter One: Where it Starts

On a gloomy day in January, the mob boss of the Crimson Eagles had a strike taken out on the Diamond Bloods Gang. Mob boss Antuninu was sitting behind his desk smoking his custom made cigar, patiently waiting for his henchmen to return. He heard someone shouting outside of his mansion, and took his trusty wheel gun out of his desk drawer.

He held the gun in his hand, and carefully pulled the hammer back and pointed it towards the door. Arlotto came barging in, and immediately froze, this is the second time that you were pointing your gun at me when I came in here, You're going to accidentally shoot someone with that one day, I know how to handle a gun.

I doubt anyone would come after you, most people are deathly afraid of you. I don't think anyone will be sneaking up on you anytime soon, and that's how I want it to be. I think that you should add a sixth man to your security team, the amount of men that I have now suits me just fine. One of your men is aging, you should think about his replacement. I'm not sure if I'm ever going to do that to him. In a demanding tone of voice he asked.

"What happened out there?"

"We sustained minimal injuries, and killed two of the rival gangs henchmen."

We set several explosive charges under two of their vehicles, with trip wires. Our inventory of explosives is running low. It's okay because I personally know someone who makes explosives and I'll be buying a lot of explosives. I personally killed one of the enemy henchmen, I shot him twice in the neck and put his body in my trunk to dispose of him later. After I take the body out of the trunk, I wipe down the inside of the trunk with a rag.

"Did he put up much of a fight?"

"Yes," he did.

He even tried to bite me, but wasn't successful

"Did anyone see you placing his body in the trunk?"

"No."

I picked up the spent bullet casings, wearing my gloves. It's the little things that may get you caught. There's blood on your shirt, it's No, big deal. Yes it is, if I were a Policeman,

I'd being questioning you about what the blood on your shirt. So next time change your shirt after doing your deed, I will keep that in mind for next time.

You should read the book "A Felons book of Ethics," that will help you not get caught by the Police. I know that you don't like to read, once you have read it bring it back to me. Keep looking me in the eyes, don't be doing anything behind my back. You don't want to know what I'd do to you.

> "Did I ever tell the story about how I caught someone stealing?"

> "Yes," you did.

I tortured that guy to death, I had no sympathy and gave him no mercy. You don't want me repeating what I did to him. What did he steal? A sliver necklace. I got it when I visited Belgium, I spent a few days there. By the look on your face you must haven't enjoyed that trip, you're right about that.

> "Have you talked to our spy Dangelo?"

> "Yes."

He said to me that he knows where the Diamond Bloods boss is.

> "What else?"

> "He says that we should go after the bosses family."

I don't think it's the right time to be doing that, we need to come up with a bulletproof plan first. He says that he already has a plan, he could've made a plan in just a day.

> "How's our ammunition supply?"

> "Good, we have one-hundred thousand assault rifle bullets and eighty thousand machine gun bullets."

> "Are our transport vehicles in good shape?"

> "Yes."

I fueled up the Lincoln, it was riddled with bullets the last time we took a hit out. You still handle that forty-four handgun pretty well, and I would never give it up.

> "How's your daughter doing?"

> "She's doing well thanks."

It will be her birthday in two days, and I know what I'll be giving her.

> "Are you going to take your daughter to dinner on her birthday?"

"No."

I thought that you enjoyed going out to the Italian restaurant, I do but who knows there could be a hit out on me. I'm afraid that my precious daughter, will be murdered. I heard that Bettino was shot in the shoulder, while on his way home a month ago.

"Do you know who attacked him?"

"The rival boss."

"Have you visited my Uncle lately?"

"Yes," I have.

He maybe old but he's still feisty.

"Did he have his cane gun with him?"

"No," he sold that.

"Now he carries a small pistol in his pants pocket, it was a light caliber."

My Uncle did meet my Grandfather, when I visit him he tells me stories about how he used go to the shooting range, and how he impressed people with his shooting. My Uncle once held up a bank, that was fifty some years ago now. He still has the gun that he used to hold up the bank.

If I remember correctly he killed two people in the bank, and wounded a third. You didn't want to mess with him while he was in his prime. Now all he can do is sit in his wheelchair, that's what age does to you.

"Will we be having a meeting tonight?"

"Yes," we are.

Tonight's meeting will be much longer than our normal meetings. I thought that Cabrini should have been back here by now. You know that he's not always on time, it's just his nature.

"Are you going to the club tomorrow evening?"

"No."

"You need to get out some more."

"Where's your daughter staying these days?"

She's currently residing in the safe house. I'm thinking about going to the Jewelry store, I'm sure your driver Tonino wouldn't mind taking you there. You haven't been there in a while, plus I'll go with you. Maybe you should swing by your daughters place and take her with you.

I'm sure you remember that one time, when I had my daughter with me when I became under fire. There were five men intently shooting at me, this happened the day before I hired you. I took a shot at one, and the bullet struck him in the side and he collapsed.

It was just two henchmen, and I can't imagine how your daughter must have felt through all that. She screamed several times when the guns went off. I'm sure she still thinks about that to this day. I gave her my gun and I said to her shoot those bad guys, but she didn't want to shoot them.

I'm not sure how you're going to break her of that, I've already broken her of that. That had really frightened her, and I don't want that happening again. As a mob boss you see a lot of killings.

My daughter has been texting me, that she's been looking for a certain bracelet. She text's me so much that it takes me awhile to read the whole message. She likes to put those funny faces in her texts sometimes.

Sometimes it's just hard to get you moving, you ponder on too much. You can worry about things while we're on our way to the Jewelry store. You don't have to listen to my suggestions. Arlotto pulled out his phone and was ready to make a call.

"Who are you calling now?"

"Your Driver"

I'm going to ask him when he thinks he can get here, I remember what happened to your last driver. He had more holes in him than Swiss cheese, one of the enemy henchman caught him by surprise, I feel bad for him. His two sons were sobbing at his funeral, his wife was so beside herself that she left before the service was over.

"Have you talked to the gold broker lately?"

"Yes."

He wants to know when you want to order again, I may order gold next week. Your driver texted me and said that he's in traffic right now, he didn't give me an arrival time. That's okay just take it easy on him, if he can't make it I'll drive then.

You would make an easier target sitting in the front of the car anyway. Hold on the driver is calling me, give me some time to talk with him. Hello Tonino, it's good to hear from you.

"What's on your mind?"

"I need help."

I just narrowly escaped, the car in front of me blew up. A gunman chased after me, I rolled down my window and returned fire at him, hitting him in the head. I backed up to where his body was lying, and opened the trunk and tossed him in and I sped off.

Before I knew it I was being followed again, but this time I was being chased by two guys on motorcycles. They opened fire on my car, lucky for me its bullet resistant.

"Did you recognize any of them?"

"No."

One of the guys had tattoos on his neck and had a scar on his forehead. They probably work for the Diamond Bloods Gang. I keep a jar full of an explosive chemical with nails in it in the console, and I threw that at them. They saw it coming but didn't have time to react, and it went off.

The one guy was engulfed in flames and crashed into a building, while the other man had nails stuck in him. I slammed my car into his bike, knocking him to the ground I didn't see him move after that. I'm tired of getting targeted by them If I have to I'll kill them all.

"Where are you at now?"

"Down by the river hiding out."

There's a man with a sniper rifle shooting at me right now. I had to crawl away from my car, to escape. He doesn't know where I am now.

"Did you hear that?"

"That's him shooting."

"Could you have Cabrini or Bettino come out and help me out of this mess?"

"Yes."

I'm looking through my binoculars at the guy, he placed his rifle in a case and ran off. Two black SUVs just pulled in besides my car, and the rival boss Tolliver just got out of the SUV and has walked over to my car.

"Can you see what he's doing?"

"Yes," I can.

He's just going through the stuff in my car, I hope that he doesn't blow it up. There are two guys with guns standing next to him, keeping watch.

"Can you get any closer to them without them spotting you?"

"No."

I'm not going to risk myself being seen by them. A third guy got out of the SUV, it's the bosses brother. I've never seen him with the boss before, it can't be good what they're planning.

One of his henchmen are wandering towards me, I'm walking further up the river. I'm standing behind a big boulder, I hope that he doesn't come back this far. Tolliver just handed his brother a gun, I wish that I knew what they were saying.

"What was all that ruckus?"

"I quickly had to move."

"Why did you move?"

"To not be seen by a guy in a boat."

I think the guy in the boat is patrolling the area for them, he's pulling up to them. You cut to conclusions way too fast, maybe he's just stopping by to say Hi. Tolliver was pouring gas over some books, and lit them on fire.

He just pulled out a loud speaker from the SUV, and turned it on. You can come out now Tonino, you won't be able to hide for much longer. You have killed a few of my men, and now I'm very angry. The henchmen are coming after me, I have to hang up bye now. You were on the phone for quite a long time, he's just in a bind right now. I don't think he'll be back by today, maybe tomorrow. I tell you what I'll drive the car, I'd like to go to the sandwich shop on the outskirts of town.

I haven't been there in quite a while, I heard that they were bought out by a new owner. I'm going to make sure that the coast is clear, before you go anywhere. Antuninu looked at the picture of his daughter that was on his desk, while waiting.

Suddenly gun fire erupted, Arlotto came running into the room. There were bullets flying all over the place out there, I narrowly escaped getting shot. I took several shots at the henchmen, I only hit two of them. There were three of them out there, one of them looked familiar to me.

I should have made head shots but I didn't, one of the guys that I shot was trying to reload his gun using one hand. He probably won't last much longer. Just excuse me for a minute while I take this last guy out, Arlotto slid the window up and climbed out.

You better find something to hide behind for cover, that's what my cars for. You started this now let's end it, I guess you aren't talking. I'm over here come and get me, the enemy henchman was standing behind his car. One of us has to fire first, who's it going to be?

Chapter Two: Holding his Own

As soon as the henchman showed himself Arlotto started firing at him, he got hit several times and collapsed in the street. Arlotto saw the injured henchman and walked over to him.

"What are you going to interrogate me?"

"No," that's not what I had in mind.

"Why don't you just shoot me?"

"No," not yet.

I have a rough idea who you're working for, you're so young to die. I should cut your head off and send it to your boss, as a little reminder.

"What do you think about that?"

"I don't know, you're scared out of your wits."

I shouldn't be wasting my time talking with you. My boss does know where your bosses daughter is, that doesn't scare me at all. Arlotto backed away and shot the man to death. He happened to look up into the sky, and saw a drone coming towards him. He fired his gun at it, and hit it twice. It crashed into one of the henchmen's cars, and exploded.

A truck came driving down the road, but he didn't see anyone in it. He had no other place to go except behind a fence. He fired on the truck, blowing out one of its tires. It was still coming for him, and exploded with enough velocity to throw him into the air. There were pieces of the truck everywhere, as he struggled to get back on his feet.

His ears were ringing and he was disoriented. He thought that he heard something and he hid behind the mansion. He peeked around the corner but didn't see anyone. His heart was racing, and he was limping. Then he realized that he was out of ammo, so he quickly ran over to his car and got some bullets from under the seat.

There was enough ammo. Not knowing what was going to happen next, he walked back to the open window and climbed in. Antuninu remarked your clothes are tore up and there's blood on your face.

"Did you feel the blast from the explosion?"

"Yes."

That explosion almost killed me, I still don't know how I walked away from it in one piece. I was able to kill the remaining henchmen.

"Did you ask him any questions?"

"Yes," but he didn't want to answer me."

You should go wash yourself up, I will when I'm ready. My main priority is keeping you safe right now. One of the henchmen mentioned to me that the rival boss knows where your daughter is. I'll gladly go get your daughter for you. Cabrini came walking into the room, with a perturbed look on his face.

"What took you so long to get here?"

"I was under attack by two gunmen."

They were firing automatic weapons, at me while I was driving away from the Fast Food restaurant. My nice car is all shot up, and I'm surprised it's still running.

It wasn't easy shooting at them on the move, but I got lucky when I hit the driver. He crashed into a diner, and got out of the car, and went over to another car and threw the driver out and got in. I parked in the alley so he wouldn't see me, he drove right past me.

"Where do you think he was headed back to?"

"Back to his place."

Bettino had called me, and said that he was at the Italian Market. He said that he was looking for something to make for dinner later. That sounds like something that he would do, one of these days someone's going to catch him off guard while he's sightseeing. I'd have to agree with you on that one. He's out in the open way too often, and I think he's getting used to it.

“Would you like some help sitting down Arlotto?”

“No,” thanks I can do it.

You look like you've been through a war, I think that you should go lay down, the best never rest. Believe me getting blown up is no fun. Cabrini opened the blinds and looked out the window, what a mess it is out there. A drone even came after me, I shot it and it came crashing down. I'm glad that it didn't crash anywhere near me.

“Was someone in that truck when it exploded?”

“No,”

“Why are you propping your leg up?”

“Because I'm looking at where I got shot.”

I'm lucky that I only got shot once. Don't worry I'm not going to pull the bullet out in front of everyone, I'll be back. He acts like getting shot is no big deal, something really serious could happen to him.

He always toughs it out, if it were me I'd be complaining the whole time. Cabrini I'd like you to go get my daughter, alright I can do that. Time is of the essence, I'm very concerned for her safety. If you need anything before I get back just give me a ring, I'll do that.

Antuninu stood up and walked down the hall to his secure gunroom. He stood back and looked at all the guns on the wall. In the corner of the room, there was a cherry cabinet. Inside the cabinet was gun cleaning supplies, he carefully pulled out the supplies. He placed his trusty gun onto a table, and picked up the rag that was on his table.

Then began cleaning it, a flashback came into his mind. It was about the time, when he was stuck in a restaurant in the middle of a gunfight. That occurred two years ago, and still hasn't left his mind. Arlotto eventually got the bullet out of his leg, and was thoroughly cleaning it.

He found a package under the sink, in the brown bag was a medical stitch kit. Within no time he began stitching himself up, and reached over and picked up the whiskey bottle and took a sip out of it. After finishing stitching himself up, he limped down the hall to see where his boss was.

When he entered the gun room it was filled with cigar smoke and there was old Italian music playing. I've never seen you so much into cleaning your guns.

“Would you shoot with me?”

"Sure I will"

"What are we shooting this time?"

"Shotguns."

We'll be shooting at some clay birds, it's just relaxing to me. We've been grimacing an awful lot, it's because I'm in pain. I still don't know how you got that bullet out of your leg so fast. I've had a lot of practice believe me.

"How longs it's been since you shot your prized shotgun?"

"A year."

"Can I carry your shotgun for you?"

"No," thanks I got it.

You can carry the box of clay birds out to the table for me. Perhaps you should bring out another box full of them, No, I never shoot a whole box. You have a lot of boxes of buckshot, that's what I use on people. Every gun that you see in here I shoot, and I keep them in good condition.

"Would you like me to go get you some iced tea?"

"No," thanks I prefer vodka.

The two men walked out to the backyard, with their guns.

"Where's the clay bird thrower?"

"Just over here."

Suddenly two men came walking in their direction, I suggest that you two back up. The two men had guns in their hands. Antuninu fired at both men killing them, they could have been on our side. I don't care whose side they were on, they were trespassing on my property.

They probably belonged to the gang, and they interrupted me. You usually smoke a cigar while you're shooting, I already smoked a big one. I'm loading the thrower as we're speaking, good now let's start shooting. The thrower tossed up one clay bird, and Arlotto missed it. Antuninu hit the clay bird, shattering it too pieces.

That right that's how you do it, it's hard for me to concentrate today. Don't give up so easy, you'll hit one sooner than later. We can worry about the bodies after we're done. I grabbed one of the dead man's wallet, that's just a waste of time. I don't have an ounce of patience with people. Someone planted a landmine in your backyard.

"Do you see where the second body is lying?"

"Yes," it's to the right of the body.

Make sure that you don't walk over there, I will.

"Do you think you could dismantle it?"

"No."

I'm sure that you know a bomb expert, just give him a call. You do the best shooting out of the two of us.

"Are you going to burn the bodies?"

"No."

We should pour acid over them, then maybe bury them. We don't want to be caught by Law Enforcement, so we must have a plan. I won't let you carry your shotgun this time, you've carried enough stuff today.

Just don't bump my gun on anything, I wouldn't do that. I'll be right back, just stay out here. Antuninu pulled out his phone and called his friend from the Bomb Squad. Hello my friend, I'm glad that you called me.

"Is there anything new with you?"

"No."

I was calling because I have a land mine in my backyard.

"How long has it been there for?"

"I'm not sure."

I haven't dared to take a closer look at it. An enemy of mine put it there. I'll be out there in an hour, just hold tight till I get there. Talk to you soon bye now, that was a quick conversation with him they usually are.

"Should we dismember the bodies?"

"No."

Don't even keep his wallet. I know where you keep your acid and gasoline.

“Would you like me to go get it?”

“Yes.”

I'll be back soon, I'm sure you'll find something to do. He sat down in his chair, and leaned back, adjusted his sunglasses and looked over at the bodies. I thought that it would be a good idea to bring out gloves too.

The drum is full of acid and is very heavy, and here's a can of gasoline. I want you to make sure that you drench the bodies in the acid, then pour the gasoline over them and light them up.

“Are you going to do the honors?”

“No,” you can do it this time.

I've burned up hundreds of bodies in my day.

“Do you think if I move the body the mine will go?”

“No.”

I would just exercise great caution while around it. This friend of mine has seen me burn bodies before, he wouldn't report us. Arlotto walked over to the first body and opened the drum and poured the acid all over the body. That looks like enough acid on the body, now pour the gasoline over it. Arlotto took a match out of his pocket, and lit it.

He threw the lit match onto the body, and it was engulfed in flames. Now come over here and sit down, you're doing a lot of work for me and I appreciate it. Arlotto said Bettino just texted me a picture of his house all shot up, he said that he wasn't home. The gang did that, he needs to find a good place to hide out in. He said that he isn't going to return home, and is currently on the move. He even has his dog with him. He just sent me a picture of his dog, this makes me miss my old dog.

“Did he say if he had any weapons with him?”

“Yes,” he did.

He just asked me where you were, I said that you're still at the mansion. It's a good thing that we didn't go to that sandwich shop, Bettino mentioned to me there was just a bomb scare there.

“Was there really a bomb there?”

“No,” there wasn't. it sure scared the people though.

The Police did show up, and had everyone evacuate the building. The people were only able to enter the shop two hours later, what a mess that is.

"How many restaurants do you own?"

"Four of them."

"Are they all Italian restaurants?"

"No," they're not.

One of them is a Steakhouse, I very rarely go there. I don't own a sandwich shop, maybe someday I will.

"Have you ever owned a gym?"

"Yes," and I still do.

A famous boxer used to train there, I met him and he's a nice guy. Him and I used to hang out at the club.

"What would you talk about with him?"

"Anything."

Just things that happened in our daily lives. My friend just texted me that he's here, I'll go get the door.

"Would you like anything from inside?"

"No," thanks I'm fine.

Several minutes later Arlotto came walking back with his friend. You look good my man, you do too. Arlotto we'll show you where the mine is, thanks.

Chapter Three: Nerves of Steel

Antuninu heard his phone ringing and answered it. It's Cabrini, I have bad news for you.

"What's that?"

"I'm surrounded by henchmen, they're all heavily armed."

They have been firing at us, and aren't letting up. We have to stay down or risk getting shot.

"How's my daughter doing?"

"She's nervous."

"Have you taken any shots at them?"

"Yes," several.

I grazed one of them and hit another one in the chest.

"Did my daughter shoot at them with her gun?"

"Yes," she did.

"Why don't you throw a grenade at them?"

"I would if I had one."

I used my last grenade two days ago. I do have a smoke grenade, I only use that in emergencies. I'm trying to get to the rifle in the cabinet, but I'm afraid I might get hit. The walls in this safe house are riddled with bullets. Your daughter just opened the cabinet, quick grab the rifle. She grabbed the rifle and handed it over to him.

"Should I let you go?"

"No," it's alright.

I have my phone on speaker phone. He aimed at one of the men and fired hitting him in the head.

"Would you let me take a shot?"

"Yes," I will.

We only have two small containers of ammo for this rifle. She took the gun from him, and when she was ready fired hitting one of the men in the shoulder. You would make a good sniper, go ahead take another shot. No, thanks. You can finish them all off.

"Do you see the man holding a bottle?"

"No," I don't.

He's the third guy on the left, I see him now. You better shoot him before he throws that, that's just what I'm going to do. He took aim and hit the guy holding the bottle, the minute that it fell out of his hands it shattered, engulfing the guy next to him on fire.

The man was flopping all over the place on the ground. Shoot the guy before he gets in his truck, I will. I just made a headshot on him. One of the men was just out of there line of sight, and fired an RPG at the house.

The house started on fire, the ceiling came down on them. We have to get out of here right now, don't worry about the gun I got that. Let's just focus on finding a way out of here, come on let's go out the back door.

"Where did you park your car?"

"It's over there, besides the bicycle and the light pole."

They quickly ran over to the car and got in.

"Do you think one of the guys saw us?"

"Yes," I do.

I think there's still two men out there. He hung up his phone, you can call him back later. Antuninu didn't hear anyone speaking into the phone and hung up. Arlotto inquisitively looked over at him.

"Who were you just talking to?"

"Cabrini"

I think I'm going to go run out for sandwiches, I'll gladly bring you back a sandwich if you want. I would like an Italian sandwich, with some chips. You can talk your friend while I'm away, see both of you later.

"How's it coming along Al?"

"It's going okay."

"Did you know that this mine is illegal in many countries now?"

"No."

You sure do know your stuff about these things.

"How many different kinds of mines are out there?"

"Thirty of them."

The mine that I'm looking at here probably cost four-thousand dollars on the black market. You can't buy any mines in Britain or you will be spending days in prison. I will have to set this mine off, so let's all come inside. I have a piece of string wrapped around the trigger mechanism, all I have to do is pull on this string and it will go off.

You're better at this than I would be, he pulled on the string and the mine went off. That was a powerful blast, it could blow a man to pieces. Weeks ago I was called out to a mine to blow up an immense boulder.

"Do you help out to bring down buildings?"

"Yes," I do.

I'll pay you fifty-thousand dollars to do a job for me.

"How soon would you need it to be done?"

"As soon as you can."

"What are you doing tonight?"

"Nothing really."

I can do it tonight for you.

"How many floors are there?"

"Two."

Three charges would bring it down, I don't think so because its fortified with concrete walls. You can't let them see you, or they will shoot you. I do carry a gun, and I recently bought a new one.

"Is there going to be people in the building?"

"Yes."

Let me guess, this is another mob-strike, yes you're correct. I'll take extra explosive charges with me, and some extra bullets for my gun. You can text me the address, and I'll program it into my navigator. The last time that you came to see me, you said to me that your brother had fallen.

"How's he doing now?"

"He made a full recovery."

"What's he been doing with his life?"

"Traveling with his girlfriend."

If you ever get bored you can become my henchman.

"Why's that?"

"Because my henchmen are always under attack, and don't stop moving."

I can't say that I ever was in a fight with another man with a gun before. I was in a few fistfights, and I won the fight every time.

"What happened to the Camaro you used to have?"

"I sold that."

I got a Chevelle SS, that's tricked out. The windows are bullet resistant, and it's hooked up to nitrous.

"How many miles are on it?"

"Eight-hundred miles."

Just then, Arlotto came walking over to them with sandwiches and bags of chips. It's very windy out there, and there weren't many people on the road. One of the roads was being worked on, so I had to take a detour. I didn't see any henchmen out there. Probably because there were some Police cars patrolling the roads.

"Were there any of the Police cars near here?"

"No."

They were a good two miles away from here. They had pulled over one person, the Officer made him get out of his car.

"What were you two talking about?"

"Explosives and mines among other things."

Arlotto handed Antuninu a sandwich along with his chips, thanks for stopping for me. Look behind you, there's a drone hovering around in your backyard. Hopefully there aren't any explosives on that drone, I see something hanging down from the drone.

I recognize that as an explosive, it's not very powerful though. Antuninu put the sandwich down and grabbed his gun firing at the drone, and exploded into pieces. These drones are getting on my nerves, we need to find the operators of these drones and shoot them. I just don't think it's safe around here for you anymore, one of these drones could come in here while you're sleeping.

The drone definitely wouldn't be able to go through my reinforced bedroom door. I think it's time for us to take your custom drone out to take a look out there.

“How's your sandwich?”

“It tastes great thanks.”

I think it's so cool that you have a gun mounted to your drone. I wanted a bigger caliber put on it but the Drone Engineers said it wouldn't fly with all that weight.

You should buy a military drone on the black market, I think I'm going to do that. I can't believe that you finished all that food already, that’s because I was hungry.

“Where are you going Arlotto?”

“To see if I can find the operators of the drones.”

I wish you luck finding them, I'm sure that I’ll need it. He walked into the backyard, and looked around. He decided to go into the woods, the high wind was blowing the trees around.

He stopped for a moment, and saw some movement off in the distance. He drew his gun, and hid behind a big tree to not be seen by whomever it was in the woods.

He was careful not to make any noise, and was careful not to step on any twigs or leaves. Now he could see the man better, the man was rigging more explosives on another drone. He was so focused on the drone that he didn't see Arlotto coming for him.

Arlotto fired at the man, hitting him twice in the chest, instantly killing him. There were two drones, and several rolls of duct tape along with a bottle of water and some trash. At the bottom of the hill there was a tent, he thought to himself I wonder if there's more guys in the woods here.

Before going down the hill he smashed the two drone with a rock that he found. He stooped down and looked into the tent, inside there was a sleeping bag a lantern and several flashlights. There weren't any guns, to his surprise.

A news helicopter flew overhead, he thought to himself I'm glad that it wasn't a military helicopter. He began his way back to the house, and soon reached the house. We heard some gunshots, and were wondering what happened.

“Did someone shoot at you?”

"No," they didn't.

I found out where the operator was, and shot him twice. I caught him in the middle of rigging up more explosives on drones.

"Did he say anything to you?"

"No," I shot him before he could say anything.

I smashed the two drones that were there. I think that you should have saved them.

"Do you think anyone else was back there?"

"I have suspicion that there is."

I saw a tent, and went through it. Just your typical camping stuff was in it, and no guns.

"Did you pick up your bullet casings when you were done?"

"No," I was being lazy.

I was wearing gloves, so I'm safe. Cabrini hasn't called me, I'm getting worried about him. Antuninu got a text from Cabrini's phone, this isn't him, but your daughter. She texted I'm sorry to say this but he's dead, he got shot several times. He texted her just call me, and she called him up.

Hello Dad, I'm sure you can hear that I'm out of breath. That's because I'm running for my life, I'm currently taking shelter in an abandoned building. I found a door in the floor that led down to a bunker.

"Did any of the gunmen see you run into the building?"

"No."

You should stay down there and don't go out anywhere. I have two guns down here with me, but I just have a bad feeling that they're going to come here and try to get me.

"What's been going on around you Dad?"

"I have been under attack."

My henchmen are making quick work of the bad guys.

"Have you had anything to eat yet?"

"No," I haven't.

"What about you Dad?"

"I had a sandwich and some chips."

"Don't you have any peanut butter crackers in your sweatshirt pocket?"

"No," I ate all of them.

I think I heard some people talking, I'm not sure how they found me. I called Bettino, and he said he can come out here. He should be here soon I would think, I'm very concerned about my safety right now.

He said to me that he knows where this abandoned building is, apparently he drove past here and seen three gunmen walking around the abandoned building.

"Did he shoot at any of them?"

"No," he didn't.

Bettino just texted me and said that he saw an armored vehicle coming down the road in my direction. He said in the text I'm sure that some henchmen are hiding inside of it.

"Were you planning on leaving the mansion dad?"

"No."

My henchmen tell me that I should leave for my own safety. They're suggesting that I should go to my lake house which is several hours away. Dad I want you to be as safe as you can. I just felt the ground shake, something must have blown up. I wish I was with you Dad.

Arlotto walked with Antuninu to his Cadillac SUV, and got in. Al came walking over to the SUV, it's nice spending time with you again. I apologize for not paying you I forgot. Arlotto knows where my safe is, just go with him and he'll give you the money.

"How much would you like to pay him?"

"Fifty grand."

Just stay in the truck I'll be back soon. He leaned back in his seat and continued talking to his daughter. He could hear some gunfire in the background, then the phone went silent.

Hello, hello, and there still was no answer. Worry immediately came into his mind, he couldn't stand the fact that he couldn't speak to his daughter anymore.

He was feeling cold so he closed the windows and turned on the heat. He opened the center console and brought out two of his pistols. He placed one of the pistols on the driver's seat, and the other one in his lap. Arlotto and Al came walking out over to the truck. Al waved to him as he was walking past.

"What's with this pistol on my seat?"

"I just wanted you to have it."

He took the pistol and placed it on the dashboard. He looked back at Antuninu, he wasn't wearing the seat belt. We may have to do some fast maneuvers, you will want to put your seat belt on this time. With a flustered look on his face he put his seat belt on.

The bodies are no longer on fire, don't worry your mansion won't burn down. They quickly sped down the driveway, I texted all your men, they know to meet us at the lake house.

We will be taking back roads, I don't want us out in the open. Meanwhile Tonino had found a row boat, and rowed across the river. Once he got to the other side, he took a look around.

Chapter Four: Uncertainty

He didn't see any gunmen, he walked a ways and came to a Fisherman's Shop. He heard engines revving nearby, and looked out at the river. Two gunmen on jet skis, were surveying the river.

One of the men, drove his jet ski onto the river bank and walked up onto the street. He saw a man walk past him and began firing his automatic weapon, at cars that drove by him. Tonino quickly ducked into the Fisherman's Shop, to take cover. The door to the back room was open, and he quickly ran into the room.

There were several spools of clear fishing line, and different sized hooks on a round table. Several fishing rods were shoved in the corner, one of them was broken in half. He almost tripped over a red bobber, and in anger kicked it out of the room.

He locked the door, and took a seat in a rustic chair. He could hear the Police sirens, and gunshots erupted. He stood up and moved the blinds away from the window and opened it and looked out. There was a Police car parked in the middle of the street, it had bullet holes down the side of it.

The windshield was shattered, and there was no sign of the Policeman. He heard someone shouting, I won't surrender to you and gunshots ensued. The gunman shouted out bring it on, he could hear the sound of a helicopter overhead.

Suddenly the back door swung open, and a man wearing a hat came in. I didn't expect anyone to be back here.

"How are you doing Sir?"

"I'm doing okay."

"Is there anything in particular that you were interested in?"

"No," there's not.

I'm just hiding out back here, from the gunman.

"What does he want with you?"

"To kill me."

The man had a surprised look on his face, I don't like the sound of that. You can stay here overnight if you'd like, no I prefer to keep moving.

"How long have you had this place?"

"For ten years."

I'm the second owner of this place, soon I'll be handing this place over to my son. The man pulled out his wallet, and took out a picture, this is my son. He's thirty-two years old, and loves to collect things.

"How much is that spool of fishing line?"

"Twenty dollars."

I'm actually a retired Police Officer, I've been retired for five years now. I have many good memories while on the job. Luckily I've never gotten shot, I was in some gunfights. I drive my boss around for a living, that doesn't sound like too much fun. I have to make sure that he doesn't get hurt.

"Must you carry a gun on your job?"

"Yes," I do.

I even drive him around at night, then you must drive him to the bars and clubs. Honestly we don't go to those places that often lately, my boss doesn't come out as much as he did before.

"Did it take you a while to get through the training?"

"No."

I just naturally love to drive, I've been driving since I've been seventeen. I tell my family that I drive a limousine around, instead of telling them I drive my boss around.

There the type that would ask me too many questions. I didn't see you pull up here in a car, I do have a car but its parked on other side of river. I don't even want to ask you why, because it's none of my business.

"Are you into classic cars by chance?"

"Yes," I am.

I have two classic cars, I've been working on them for a year. I would love to continue talking with you, but I have to get on my way. Just be careful out there, I will thanks. He opened the door and walked out, the Police Officer was lying in the street in a pool of blood.

He thought to himself the gunman must be hiding around here somewhere. He saw that there was a big truck pulled over, and walked over to it. The driver immediately rolled down the window, and looked at him.

"What are you doing here Sir?"

"To ask you a question."

"Are you an Uber driver?"

"Yes."

I need you to drive me to a location.

"Is this location in this state?"

"Yes," it is.

The last guy had me drive him for two hours, and I hit traffic. This guy in traffic, threw a rock at my truck and I just got a new paint job on this truck too. You don't have to stand there you can get in now. When he opened the door some magazines fell out, don't worry about them let them lay.

He picked them up anyway, and put them under the seat and got in the truck. I like the leather interior, that's part of the reason why I bought this truck. You've got some big tires on this thing, that's just how I like it.

Each tire cost me thousands of dollars. I have a shotgun in this truck, I didn't see it when I got in here. Whenever you're ready you can tell me the address, it's 349 Blazer Street, 17776. I have never been to that place.

"Is it nice?"

"Yes."

"Do You personally live there?"

"No," I don't.

"Is someone having a party there?"

"No," it's just a friend of mine.

"How long have you been driving people around?"

"Just over two years."

"Have you had much go wrong with this truck?"

"No," I don't have any complaints.

After I drive you to your location, I'm going to get an oil change. If you want some water just asked me for some, I'll do that.

"Have you gone hunting this year?"

"No," my job is very demanding,

I don't have time for that.

"Where did you pick this truck up at?"

"Trucks Unlimited."

There's some traffic on the highway.

"Would you be alright with me going on the back roads?"

"Yes."

Suddenly a car swerved into their lane, I don't know what that guys problem was.

"Was that man armed?"

"No," not that I could see.

He slammed on the brakes when the light turned red. I have taken my truck off roading, and that was so much fun. I drove it through the farmers field, I'm surprised that you didn't get stuck. That cats lucky that it didn't get run over crossing the street. You have a worried look on your face, I swear I saw someone standing on the side of the road with a gun.

"What was he wearing?"

"A trench coat."

I couldn't see his face. I don't want my truck getting shot up, or me getting killed. It's almost as dark as night out here, it's probably going to rain at any moment. If you want to take a break driving I'll drive for a while, No, thanks I'm fine.

"Is there someone after you Sir?"

"No."

We have to stop, there's a tree lying across the road. This looks like some kind of setup to me, you better be sure that no one's after you. He handed the shotgun, you shoot anyone that looks suspicious. I'm going to get my chainsaw out of the back of the truck, it shouldn't take me long. This truck has a nice long bed, everything's in order back here.

"What's in the small box?"

"Extra chains for the chainsaw."

He picked up the chainsaw and started it up and walked over to the tree with it. We're lucky this isn't going to take long to clear. Keep your eyes out for anyone coming this way, I'm depending on you to save us. He cut the tree up into several pieces and pushed them off the road.

Don't move there's a four legged robot walking this way, there appears to be a rifle on its back. Tonino began firing at it, go ahead and keep shooting it until it falls over. This thing has some plate armor on it, I'm not sure if this buckshot will go through it.

Quick get behind my truck, nothing looks like it means business. The robot began firing it's weapon at them. You better hope this robot doesn't blow up your truck. Be quiet a minute, it stopped moving. I got a good shot at it from here, and he took the shot.

The robot walked a little closer to him and fell over, and exploded. You can get in the truck awhile, I'm just finishing up putting my chainsaw away. He feverishly got into his truck, and they took off. I don't want to see another one of those things, now I'm on high alert.

You haven't mentioned to me how much this ride will cost. Because I prefer for you to pay me when we get there, that's fair enough. This road has many twists and turns to it.

I can't see the middle yellow line because of the fog. I've doing sixty-five mph, and I'm going to slow down. He happened to look in his rearview mirror, and saw an driverless motorcycle behind him.

“What did you see in your mirror?”

“A driverless motorcycle.”

You must be joking or something, just look in your side mirror and you'll see it. I see it now, this is definitely something new. It's doing pretty good keeping up with us. If it gets any closer I'm going to slam my truck into it. I saw some explosives on that bike, we can't be fooling around with this thing.

A crow flew into the truck and bounced off of their windshield. That bike is coming up on your side, I wouldn't shoot if I were you there's a chance it may blow up.

“What do you suggest to do?”

“Pull over.”

I don't think pulling over is a very wise idea. He put the truck into four wheel drive, and drove it off the road. Look it's no longer following us, watch that deep divot. He stopped the truck completely, I'm wondering if this dirt road will take us back onto the main road again.

I don't see why not, just keep following it. This is turning into an adventure, I haven't been on an adventure for so long. When I get back home I'm going to tell my girlfriend about all this, she probably won't believe it. We should have done something to take out that motorcycle, it's too late now.

If I see that thing again I'm just going to shoot it, I don't care if it blows up. I've taken many risks before, and nothing happened to me. There's a four wheeler coming this way, you may want to pull over and see what he wants.

At this pace it will take us all day to get there. He stopped the truck and let down the window, the man got off of his bike and came over. These are game lands, you weren't doing the speed limit, you better think about slowing down.

"Do you need something with us?"

"No," I just wanted to tell you that.

"Please don't give us a hard time."

"Are you a Game Warden?"

"No," I'm not.

"Have you saw any deer around here?"

"Yes," I've seen two bucks.

You guys have a safe trip I'll talk to you later, and he sped off. That guy certainly wasn't very pleasant, he's got a short fuse. I thought he was going to give you a fine or something, me too. I wouldn't want to spend my day with him. I don't think he's around a lot of people very often, don't make excuses for him. I want to go faster but I don't trust my driving, these trees are closer to us than we think they are.

I can always drive, I may take you up on that soon, there's mud splashed up all over your truck on this side, that doesn't matter. Don't point that out again, focus on the area around you. I saw some wild turkeys back there.

"How many were there?"

"Four of them."

One of my headlights just went out. Your hands are awfully shaky on the steering wheel, that's because I'm nervous. I like how these windows are tinted, it cost me a pretty penny.

"Does this road show up on your GPS?"

"Yes," it does.

It shows that we are another twenty-two minutes out. We still have made good time getting here. Eventually they reached the front gate, and it was open. He drove right in, there are many other vehicles here. That's okay because I know those people. It was great having you with me, likewise.

"How much is it?"

"Eighty-five dollars."

He pulled out his wallet and took out the money and gave it to the man, thanks a lot I appreciate it. The man waved to him as he was leaving. Arlotto came walking out, we thought something tragic happened to you.

“Where's Antuninu?”

“He's sitting on the back deck looking over the lake.”

That's a nice place to be, I'm tired and I need some rest.

“Where's Cabrini?”

“I'm afraid he was killed.”

We'll be attending his funeral in two weeks, I would have liked to say goodbye to him.

“What's Bettino doing?”

“He's trying to get Antuninu's daughter out of harm's way.”

I just got a text from him, it's not good. He said to me, that the boss's daughter was taken by a henchman, and that he's got a knife injury from fighting off one of the henchmen.

“Is he on his way here?”

“No.” he's going back after them.

How about you come inside, that sounds good.

“Would you like some whiskey?”

“No,” thanks.

Alcohol seems to slow me down, I think I'm going to take a smoke. I'm sure that Antuninu, would like your company why don't you go sit with him. Since his daughter was taken I don't think he's going to be in a good mood. Suddenly they heard shooting coming from the back deck, I wonder what just happened. The both men walked into the yard, Antuninu was looking out at the lake.

“What were you shooting at boss?”

“A floating log in the lake.”

“Did you hit it?”

“Yes,” several times.

"Would you like another cigar?"

"Yes," I would.

A pigeon flew over and he shot it down, now that's what I call a good shot. He looked back at Tonino, it's a nice surprise seeing you here. I spent my day being shot at again.

"What can I do to get your daughter back?"

"Kill some more henchmen."

The other gang better not kill my daughter. they're probably tying her up right now. It makes my blood boil knowing that they have her. Could you bring me my binoculars, Yes I will. Arlotto brought the boss his binoculars, he immediately began looking into them, I see a black truck parked in the woods.

Arlotto grabbed his gun off the picnic table, I'll go take a look for you. I think that whomever it is, is hiding under the water. There probably wearing there wetsuit and scuba diving equipment. Any minute now he may come up out of the water and attack us.

Chapter Five: Incoming

We need to get away from the lake, they walked away from the lake and went inside. You can sit on the couch Tonino, No, thanks I'd like to stand. You never know when we're going to be attacked.

They were all looking out the window at the lake, a scuba diver came walking out of the lake, holding a speargun. Arlotto opened the window and started firing at the man, and hit him twice killing him.

"Do you think there's more men in the lake?"

"Yes," I do.

Just give them some time they're come out, they might wait until tonight to come out. No, I don't think so. We need to take out your drone out to see what's happening. The battery isn't charged, then we'll charge it.

"Where's the drone?"

"It's in the cabinet over there, that's against the wall."

I'll work on the drone, you guys can keep looking out the window. Someone just threw a smoke grenade, it's a good thing we aren't out there. I wouldn't go out there Tonino, I ain't going to just stand here and watch your property get destroyed. These henchmen don't know who there're messing with.

I'm wearing a bulletproof vest, so I'm not afraid. He stormed out the back door, hopefully he comes back in one piece. This isn't like him, he's usually more easygoing. He's been going nonstop, No, wonder he's acting like this. We heard you sigh and groan.

"Is everything okay with the drone Arlotto?"

"Yes"

I forget how these wires plug into the battery of the drone. Just try to clear your mind for a minute and try again. That's what I've been trying to do, it's not working for me.

"Do you know anything about these batteries?"

"I'm afraid that I don't."

Gunfire broke out, hopefully Tonino made a good shot. That black truck that I was looking at earlier just blew up. I'm surprised that I don't have PTSD from all this. Tonino came into the room, I just killed two more henchmen. I'm so tired that I'm going to fall over. I'll be resting in the bedroom if anyone needs me, and he slammed the bedroom door shut.

"Where did you get that energy bar?"

"From The kitchen"

"Would you like one?"

"Yes," I would.

I'll go get one right now.

"Do you see anything going on out there?"

"No."

He carefully handed his boss the bar, thank you. Just let me know if you'd like another one. He dropped the bar, and his jaw dropped. Come quick, a small object just came up out of the water. That's an underwater drone, look there's duct tape wrapped around it.

That means that there's a bomb strapped to it. It must be a heavy bomb because it's moving slow. We can't just sit here and talk about it. Please get away from the window, I have to get in there.

I'm going to use the AR that's standing up in the corner to shoot the drone. Hold your ears, Arlotto fired at the drone, hitting it twice. It exploded, and a piece of it came flying through a side window. Tonino came out of the bedroom, with a dazed look on his face. Of course something happened when I went to lay down.

"What were you shooting at now?"

"At another drone."

Let me guess it had a bomb on it, yes it did. I feel like I'm living in a war zone, all I want to do is sleep. If there was sand in here I'd put my head in it.

"Did you lock up the front gate?"

"Yes."

All we would need is for someone to come through there after us. Instead of sleeping in the bedroom, l may go down into the bunker and sleep there. I swear every minute you're under attack, but at this rate we'll all fall over from exhaustion. I swear our enemy has unlimited henchman, were probably close to killing most of them.

Alright fellas I'm going to go down into the bunker now, talk to you later. Tonino cracks me up, he always says something funny. I haven't seen him that tired in a while. I finally got the drone charging, that really tested my patience. The drone is dusty so I'm wiping it down, you don't need to do that.

"Who put this thing away last?"

"Bettino."

He doesn't exactly put things back the way he found them. Arlotto picked up his phone and saw a text message from Bettino. He quickly went into his messaging app, and saw that Bettino had texted him three times. Bettino said that he's watching the enemy gang from a far at their Headquarters.

Arlotto quickly texted him back, asking him where Antuninu's daughter was. He replied by saying, she's somewhere inside the gangs Headquarters. Antuninu was watching Arlotto, as he was looking over the drone.

We'll be able to fly it tonight if you're lucky. I know where you're daughters being held.

"Where at?"

"The gangs Headquarters."

I suggest that we attack that place tonight, besides that at night there's less guards that we have to worry about.

"What weapon are you going to be carrying?"

"My custom AR."

I found a wooden box under a table full of grenades, I'll be taking some of them with me tonight. Dangelo just sent me a virtual map, of the Headquarters of the Diamond Bloods Gang. I can see what's currently going on there in real time.

I just counted five guards around the place, I'm sure there are trip wires all around that place. I've always been good at seeking out trip wires. There's someone lying on the ground all tied up. I'm hoping that it's not your daughter, me too. Meanwhile Al, had just arrived at the location, there were three guards wearing bullet proof vests and holding there assault rifles. One of the guards was opening up a garage. From where he was standing he couldn't see what was inside. He just figured that there was a car in there, and went on with his business.

He grabbed his gear bag and ran around to the back of the place, when he saw one of the guards coming he ducked back behind a tall hedge. Two of the guards began talking to one another, another guard lit up a cigarette. Now the guards weren't looking back at the house, he took his chance and ran up to the front door.

He quickly took out the lock picking tool from his pocket, and began picking away at the door. Eventually he was able to open the door. He quickly entered, from where he was standing he could see a guard. He wasn't sure which way he was headed, and ducked behind the couch. He could hear the guard speaking into his walkie talkie, everything is good in here.

Al went into the kitchen, he pulled out his knife. When the guard walked into the kitchen, Al stabbed him in the throat, and the guard collapsed into a puddle of his own blood. He began searching for the basement door, to his surprise the door was open. He went over to the body, and dragged it over to the top of the steep basement steps.

He gave the body a shove and it went down the steps. He wasn't sure if there were any guards in the basement, so he preceded with caution. He found a light switch and switched on the lights, and found a place to set the charges. He got to work setting up the charges, it didn't take him long to set them up.

Once he was done he could hear footsteps above him, he quickly turned off the lights. He could hear the guard saying, I found some blood on the kitchen floor, the guard was looking at the bloody drag marks that lead down into the basement. So he decided to go down to the basement, when he got to the bottom step, Al came out and cut the guards throat, the guard fell down face first. He knew that he didn't have much more time to get out of there. He darted up the steps and closed the door behind him. He went down the hall and came upon the master bedroom. He quickly entered the room, and went under the bed.

Where he placed the charges, he quickly got out from under the bed. He proceeded into a backroom, where he put his final charge. He could hear one of the doors opening nearby. Once the final charge was ready he left the room, to find a way out. He thought to himself how many rooms does this place have.

The guard shouted out, I know someone's in here now come out. Al thought to himself I'm going to have to take a risk to get out of here. He sprinted towards the open front door, quickly exiting the place.

The guard that was by the garage saw him running away, and began chasing after him. Al ducked into an alley hoping to escape the guard, but somehow he was still behind him.

Al took out his pistol and fired at the guard. The guard hid behind the dumpster, he shouted out you're a terrible shot. I'd like to know what you were doing there, you don't need to know why. All I'm doing is what I was asked to do, by my boss.

"What were you looking at in that garage?"

"Something that you don't need to know about."

The guard exposed himself and Al took the opportunity to take a shot at him, hitting him once in the side and in the chest. Al soon came upon his car, and texted Antuninu before getting in his car. He pressed in the detonator and the building exploded. An hour later, he got home safely. Antuninu, put his feet up and was relaxed. While Arlotto was setting up the tablet to fly the drone. He could hear a lot of huffing coming from Arlotto. I'm burning some brain cells over here, the tablets saying that it needs to be updated, this thing always takes a while to update.

It's telling me that it's going to take an hour to update, that doesn't sound so bad. It's an hour since Tonino has laid down, I'm sure he's just fine. A few hours later, Antuninu and Arlotto got themselves ready to go.

Tonino still didn't wake up. I don't care what Tonino says I'm waking him up, he went down the steps and opened the door to the bunker and went down into it. To his surprise he was sitting up, I was just coming down to wake you up. We're going to head out soon.

"Does your gun still have plenty of ammo in it?"

"Yes," it does.

Here's a new clip for your gun anyway, you can just let the other clip on the floor. They walked up the steps back into the house, and exited through the front door. It took them some time to load up the truck, with extra ammunition along with some explosives.

Don't forget to put on your bulletproof vest, we won't. Tonino turned the truck on, Arlotto got out and opened the gate and after they went past it he closed it up. My phones GPS said we'll be there in two hours. I thought that they were further away than that.

Arlotto was sitting in the back comfortably next to Antuninu, holding his gun. Two hours later, they we're at the Headquarters. We're going to park the truck at the gas station over here, so that they don't see us.

I'm going to set off a bomb, over there in the empty parking lot, to keep their attention away from us. Alright Arlotto, you go ahead and do that. I can see Bettino over there hiding behind a food truck. Tonino and Antuninu, hid behind a statue that was nearby to the Headquarters.

> "Do you think anyone saw us come over here?"

> "No," I don't think so.

> "Are you going to take the first shot?"

> "No," you can.

I don't even see anyone to shoot. A Police car drove down the road nearby to them.

> "Doesn't seeing that Police car make you nervous?"

> "No."

Tonino, peeked around the corner and saw a henchman coming out of the Headquarters building. I just saw a man come out of the building.

> "Which way is he headed?"

> "Not this way."

Let me know when he's coming this way.

> "Can you still see where Arlotto went?"

> "Yes," he's still standing in the parking lot.

I didn't hear a bomb go off either, perhaps something went wrong with the bomb. Look he's running away from the lot, suddenly the bomb went off. Three men stormed out of the Headquarters, holding their assault rifles with an angered look on their faces. Watch out one of the men are coming towards us, Get prepared to shoot. The minute the henchman came around the corner Antuninu fired his gun at the man, hitting him in between the eyes. There's a man coming for you now, Tonino opened fire on the man and he collapsed.

Quick let's get behind that truck that's parked closer to the Headquarters, they rushed over by the truck. I think we might be too close to the building, no I think we're all right.

I haven't seen anyone come out of the building in a while. We must have exhausted all the men that there are. I'm sure there's some more men somewhere around here, waiting to surprise us. They won't be surprising either one of us, I can't wait to shoot more of the men.

"Do you see Arlotto at the other side of the Headquarters?"

"Yes," I do.

He better take cover before he gets shot, there's two henchmen shooting at him. I'm sure that he can handle them just fine, he knows it's out to fend off the enemy. He just took out the two henchmen, look here comes a surveillance drone, it soon came into range and Antuninu shot it down.

You're getting to be an old pro at shooting the drones down, there's a drone hovering over by Arlotto. I'm sure that he will see it eventually and shoot it down. Arlotto turned around, and saw the drone and quickly shot it down. A big black swat team truck was coming down the road, the sewer cap in the street is open let's retreat down there.

Chapter Six: Clash of the Titans

They both climbed down into the sewer, it smells awful down here. Several rats went scurrying past them, we need to keep moving so that we don't get caught. I don't think we'll get caught right away, they still don't know that we're down here. Arlotto won't tell them where we're at, hopefully he's able to hide from the Swat Team.

"Who do you think called the Swat Team?"

"Some concerned people."

I didn't see many people on the streets. When I shot that drone down I saw a driver speed past us, I think the person was terrified after hearing the gun shot.

"How far down from here do you think this sewer ends?"

"A few miles maybe more."

You wouldn't want to walk to the end of the sewer. I hear some commotion from above, I wouldn't worry about it. Let's take a right down here, I'm not going to get us lost. Were under the Headquarters right now, I'm sure that hatch opens up and leads up into the Headquarters.

But with the Swat Team walking around we don't want to be in that building right now. Anyone in that building will probably be arrested, I've never seen the Swat Team come up out to a location so fast.

Suddenly multiple gunshots went off, those shots sound like they came from the Headquarters above. I'm wondering who's doing all that shooting, It could Arlotto. I'm sure that he's probably in the Headquarters by now. It's not easy these days hiding from the law or hiding from the surveillance drones in the cities.

"How many surveillance drones do you think are in the city?"

"Four of them."

The most recent surveillance drones have small guns on them that shoot rubber projectiles. They use these drones to keep the protesters under control.

"Who's in charge of controlling the drones?"

"By Private Security Contractors."

I can't believe that the Government uses the people's tax money to buy surveillance drones. I myself don't like to be watched by drones.

"How many hours of recordings can these drones do?"

"Several hours."

This water we're treading through is black, and smells like rancid milk. I wish that we could get out of here right now, but I'd rather be down here than get caught. I wouldn't want to be locked up in a small jail cell for the rest of my life. They came to a two way intersection, let's take a right here.

"Do you hear that water splashing?"

"Yes."

It sounds like they're coming this way, we'll see who it is very soon. I think it's another henchman coming for us, you could be right. Tolliver came walking around the corner, both of the men had their guns pointed at him. I can't believe that I run into you too, what an adventure it's been. You always have that stern look in your face Antuninu.

"What did you do with my daughter?"

"Nothing yet."

I don't believe that at all, your just lying. For all I know she could have a noose around her neck, ready to get hung. I would do something much worse to her than that. I got my dual pistols on me, and I'll shoot the both of you to pieces. I know that you're just all talk, and not much action.

"Where are your men to protect you?"

"Your henchman killed them all."

I don't believe that for a minute, they're around here somewhere. If you reach into your pocket I'm going to shoot. You're the one who's going to be in a pool of your own blood. You think talking tough will scare me, I haven't been afraid of you since day one. I have your daughter at my private residence, and she's tied up lying on the floor in my living room.

I kicked her a couple times for screaming, Her scream gave me a headache, she tried to fight back but I overpowered her. I tore the necklace off of her neck, and cut off her bracelet. I gave her a punch to the mouth. When I left your daughter was crying and whimpering. Your daughters face is bloody, from getting beaten.

Antuninu was clenching his fist, you're going to pay for this with your life. My girlfriend is currently with her, all I have to say is kill her and she will. I don't believe that any of your henchmen know where my place is, I bet they do. You've always had a big mouth on you, and you don't.

I'm tired of even looking at you, what you did to my daughter is wrong. You don't need to keep talking to me you can shoot me if you want. In case you didn't know it I have a private spy, and he's scoped out your place before. I had no idea about that, I was told by one of my henchmen that your henchman Cabrini was killed in the heat of a battle. He was just a pathetic person, and not much of a fighter. Your partner there's a coward, he was hiding from me and my guys.

"Where were you hiding Tonino?"

"I was hiding in a Fisherman's Shop."

That's just laughable, only a coward would do that. I'm surprised that you haven't come back at me with a comment yet. I don't waste my time arguing with anyone, you're no different. You should have fault my men, instead of running from them. You better not run from me or I'll shoot you in the back.

You shouldn't shoot a man in the back, now that's what a coward would do. You have no room to talk about that, of course I do. I'm probably a faster shooter than you are, I liked you better before you opened your mouth.

After we kill you, we will be going after your brother. You won't be able to find him, he's probably in a bunker somewhere. He can run but he can't hide from us. I'll ask my spy to find him, he's my secret weapon.

"Where's your man Arlotto?"

"He's looking for more of your men to kill."

Suddenly a swat team guy came down into the sewer, Tolliver opened fire on the man. He was riddled with holes, and collapsed. I don't care about law enforcement, all they do is slow me down. I'm not afraid to kill anyone, I'm a cruel man. As Tolliver was reloading Antuninu opened fire on him, and so did Tonino. The bullets tore through Tolliver's bulletproof vest, two bullets struck him in the legs and in the jaw. His body went limp and he fell over into the rancid water, I'm glad that he's gone. I'm not sure what to do with these bodies, there's not much you can do with them.

I'm sure someone will find these bodies and bury them, the bodies will decay before their found. There's probably homeless people that live down here, I haven't seen any yet so I don't believe that theory.

Tonino kicked a dead mouse out of their way, I would have shot that mouse out of the way. I can hear a Police siren, it won't be easy to avoid Law Enforcement now.

Above the street, the street was littered with dead Swat Team Officers. People were running for their lives, there was a car that sped down the street. The driver was driving carelessly, and ran over one of the dead bodies and crashed into a pole. The driver ran out of his car and ran down the street. Arlotto looked around for henchman, and didn't see any so he preceded back to the truck and got in.

He feverishly opened up the duffel bag that was on the floor, and took the clip out of his gun and began reloading it, with the bullets that were in the bag. Somewhere in the crowd of scared people there was an active shooter, the man shot at two people who were running away from him, hitting one of them.

Arlotto thought to himself I can't in good conscious let that guy keep shooting at people. Once his gun was fully loaded, he got out of the truck and began searching for the gunman. Soon he caught up with the man, excuse me Sir you're coming with me. Arlotto wrestled with the man, knocking him to the ground.

People were watching the two men go at it, one of the people that was watching them threw an empty bottle at them. I'm not going to shoot you in front of all these people, come back here behind this building.

The minute the man came back there, he shot him dead. He threw the man's body over his shoulder, and walked down the street until he came to the truck.

He opened up the back of the truck and threw the body in it. He looked over at the street, and saw an Swat Team Officer's body. He went over to the body, the man was just too heavy to lift. He dragged the body over to his truck, and gave it his all throwing it into the back of the truck.

With sweat pouring down his forehead he slammed the door shut. The Swat Team truck was parked nearby, he quickly walked over to it and decided to get into it. There were two assault shotguns inside, along with several smoke grenades. He put one of the smoker grenades in his pocket and took one of the shotguns with him. He preceded back to the truck and got in.

He thought to himself I'm wondering what's taking the guys so long to get back here. A while later Antuninu Tonino came up out of the sewer, and were now on their way back to the truck. Eventually they got to the truck, and got in. I'm glad that the both of you are okay, We killed Tolliver, he came after us while we were in hiding.

We shot him to pieces, and don't regret it. Now I have to get back to his place to get my daughter, who's being held there by his girlfriend she's going to get a rude awakening.

Dangelo texted me and said that he's there, he already killed the woman that was holding your daughter. Then he texted me that he was headed back to the lake house.

       "How long ago did you get that text?"

       "Twenty minutes ago."

Text Dangelo and ask him if he knows, where Tolliver's brother lives. We're going to pay him a visit, that's a nice shotgun that you got there Arlotto. I took it from the Swat Team truck.

       "Have you shot it yet?"

       "No," I haven't.

I just got a text back from Dangelo, were in luck he knows his address. He just texted me his address now, and I'm putting it into my phone's navigator. It says that were forty-five minutes out from the destination.

Take a right here on Silverton Rd, after a mile you'll want to turn left on Bulldog Rd. It's suggesting that we should get on the highway, just ignore it. There's a lot of people out on the street, it looks like they're having a get together or something. Look at all those kids at the playground, they're just having a grand old time.

“Did you see that guy that looks suspicious wearing the hoodie?”

“Yes.”

Please pull over for a moment, I don't like how he's looking at the kids. I'm afraid that he's going to kidnap one of them, now don't cut to conclusions just yet. Antuninu it's not worth it to shoot him, we should be on our way now. Let's go then, we can't just keep stopping. You better slow down or you'll have the Police after us.

“Would you like to take over driving?”

“No,” thanks.

I don't know how we got stuck behind a trash truck, he's going slower than the speed limit. Just pass him, were in a no passing zone.

“Where's that foul odor coming from?”

“From the back.”

He looked at Arlotto, I think that you put dead bodies in here again. I'll get them out, once were at our destination. You should look out the windows for a bit and try to relax.

You know that I don't like to do that, I'm always on high alert. There's a guy behind us on a motorcycle revving his engine, it's just some adrenaline junkie. He just passed us doing a wheelie, so what.

“Do you think his brother is expecting us?”

“No.”

The GPS says turn right here into the apple orchard, just do what it says. I don't see any other houses around here, who would want to live in an apple orchard to begin with. One of the apple trees is cut down, look there's an old road sign. There's an antique motorcycle parked in front of that barn over there. I never saw a wind mill so close to a house before.

"Do you think he lives off grid?"

"I'm not sure."

"What if he's not home?"

"Then we will go looking for him."

What a long driveway he has, I can't believe that he don't have his driveway paved, not everyone likes to do that. I just heard a rooster crow, I never heard one of those crow in a while. There sure is a lot of shade back here, but that sun is hot. I hope that he doesn't have guard dogs, it's no big deal if he does.

You just stepped on a few apples getting out, I don't care. There's a truck parked in the driveway, it's most likely his. We're going to attack the place from the back, just shadow me while I walk back here.

They saw the curtain move and opened fire, Antuninu took out a cigar from his pocket, and brought out his lighter, and lit it. Arlotto was standing at the front of the place.

Antuninu said to Tonino, one of us needs to go inside. Tonino immediately went over to the back door and kicked it in. He could hear someone moaning in pain.

He walked down a hall and saw that the bedroom door was open. A man was laying down on his back in front of his bed. His clothes were all bloody, and he had a wound on his arm. The man looked over at him, he looked drowsy.

"Are you Tolliver's brother?"

"Yes," I am.

I wasn't expecting anyone to come here today, I was in the kitchen trying to eat my sandwich when you guys opened fire on me. I got shot in the arm, and a bullet grazed my leg.

I wasn't asking for any trouble, it doesn't matter your part of the gang. It's over for your gang now, we killed your leader. The man began to sob, I can't believe that this is happening.

I don't even have my gun on me. The man quickly reached under his bed and grabbed his gun. Tonino shot the man dead, and began going through the rooms. In one of the small rooms, there were some ammo cans stacked on one another. Against the back wall, was a small cabinet with three drawers.

He opened the first drawer and found a baggie full of drugs, along with needles. He looked over at the closet and saw that there was a tripwire in front of it. He exited the room, and entered the next one. In this room there was, bars of silver and gold.

There were two posters on the wall, and a shotgun was leaning against the wall. He left this room end entered a small bedroom, where a young woman was lying on the floor. He spoke to her but she never answered, there were needle marks in her arms and part of her face was black and blue.

He checked her for a pulse, but there wasn't one. After that he quickly got out of the place, he was shocked by what he saw. Antuninu saw Tonino storm out the back door.

"Are you alright?"

"Yes," I am.

I heard a gunshot from inside, I shot his brother dead. I have reason to believe that he's a drug addict, because I found a lot of drugs and needles. I found the body of a young woman in one of the bedrooms. She had needle marks all over her, and her face was black and blue.

He must have beat her or something, this place is a wreck inside. I don't know how people can live like this. In the one room I found a lot of ammunition. He tried to make me feel sorry for him, but it didn't work and I shot him.

You won't believe what I found out here in the yard. I found three shallow graves. This man was a killer, but now he's gone thanks to you. Arlotto came walking over to them, I was wondering what you guys were doing back here. We're just talking about what we found around here.

"Did you find any drugs in there?"

"Yes."

He went for his gun and I shot him.

"Were there any bodies inside?"

"Yes," just one.

"Did you find anything out of the ordinary out front?"

"Yes," I did.

There were tripwires wrapped around two apple trees.

“Did you happen to venture over to the barn?”

“No.”

I was going to leave that up to you too.

“Do you think the old bike would start up?”

“No.”

The men went walking towards the barn, stop a minute. The ground looks different over there, I see what you mean. Don't walk over that area, it's not safe. One of them picked up a rock and threw it onto the ground, and it exploded. A big cloud of dust went up into the air, I wasn't expecting such an explosion.

“Do you think that motorcycle is booby trapped?”

“Yes.”

“Are you going to shoot it?”

“Yes,” to see if it blows up.

He shot at the motorcycle, hitting it and it exploded. Pieces of the bike flew everywhere, look there's a fender over there. One of its tires flew over there by our truck. That was such a nice bike too, don't worry you'll find another one like that someday.

“Do you have any favorite kind of bike?”

“No,” I like them all.

Look the barn is on fire now, I don't care about the barn, let it burn. Whatever belongs to that rotten guy can burn. To their surprise a horse came running out of the barn, it's coming over to you Arlotto.

The horse was now close enough for him to pet it. I've never owned a horse before, probably because I don't have the time. It surely seems to like you, animals seem to be attracted to me.

“Are you going to ride him?”

“No,” we don’t have the time for that.

If you get on horses back, we’ll take your picture. No, thanks I'm not interested. Arlotto went over to one of the apple trees, and picked an apple off of it and took a bite out of it.

“How's that apple taste?”

“It tastes good.”

You should try one, I think I will.

“Have you ever drank hard cider?”

“Yes,” I have and it's good.

Antuninu was leaning up against the front of the truck, smoking his cigar. He really enjoys his cigars, that's okay let him enjoy it. I could really drink a cold beer right now.

Arlotto picked up an apple and gave it to the horse. You better watch your fingers while feeding the horse, don't worry I am. I almost lost a finger feeding a horse, I was just a kid when it happened.

“Do you think the police are looking for us out here?”

“No.”

I barely get any reception back here on my cell phone.

“Do you think the horse is going to follow us out of here?”

“No,” he'll just runoff.

I want to blow up the man's truck, you don't need to do that. Suddenly a plane flew overhead, there's not a cloud in the sky. It would be a great day to skydive, I've done it three times.

I think all three of us should go sky diving. Antuninu got in the truck and so did Tonino. Arlotto petted the horse one last time, and got in the truck. You really took a real liking to that horse, Yes I know. When they pulled out the horse bolted away in the opposite direction.

“Are you all ready to get out of here?”

“Yes,” we are.

“Do you want to take some apples with?”

“No.”

I put in the address of the lake house, and we're ready to go. Be careful not to back up into that apple tree.

“Do you think the Detectives are investigating the deaths of the Swat Team Officers?”

"Yes."

"How long do you think it will take them to finish the investigation?"

"A week or two."

I'm sure once we leave this orchard there will be Police and Investigators all over it. It won't be easy for them to figure out who shot the man, because my fingerprints aren't on the bullet. It will feel good to rest when we get back. I'm glad that we're finally off of this dirt road, now we can go faster. A car sped past them, that driver's going too fast.

Suddenly the driver slammed on the brakes, and pulled off the road. A gunman got out of the car, and started firing at them. Arlotto immediately went into action, and put the window down and start firing back at the gunman. He hit the gunman in the head, and they drove off. That was a real close call, No, it wasn't that bad.

"Do you think we'll come upon a gas station soon?"

"Yes."

I just ran out of water, I'm going to buy several bottles of water. They soon came upon a gas station, Arlotto got out of the truck and entered the store, while Tonino was filling up the truck with gas. Antuninu remained sitting in the truck, looking out the windows. Tonino went into the store to pay for the gas, while Arlotto was paying for the water. A few minutes later they both came out, I'm sure glad that the line in there was short. I don't like to wait in lines, the hoagies in there don't look so appetizing. Arlotto took the bodies, out of the back of the truck. He shoved the bodies into an old rusty truck that was behind the station and covered them with a tarp. Tonino saw what he was doing, and struck up a conversation with him.

"Have you ever tried there fresh Turkey wraps?"

"Yes," and they were good.

"Do you get a certain brand of water?"

"No," I buy whatever brand they have.

Tonino, got in the truck and kept to himself. They got back on the road, I've been seeing a lot of tractor trailers going down this road. Hopefully we aren't on this road for very long. Arlotto let out a yarn, all of the action has made me tired. After several hours they reached the lake house, Bettino met them there with Antuninu's daughter with him. His daughter ran over to him and hugged him, with tears in her eyes. I'm glad to be back Dad, I thought that those guys we're going to kill me. Just take it easy, I love you Dad, I love you too. Eventually all of them decided to lay down for the night. The very next day, they flew the drone around. It's fun to sit around flying this drone, they all took turns flying it. They stayed at the lake house for the rest of the day.